THE LITTLEST PIRATE AND THE HAMMERHEADS

NICHOLAS NOSH MAY BE THE LITTLEST PIRATE IN THE WORLD, BUT HE'S ALSO THE **BRAVEST**. WHEN EVIL CAPTAIN HAMMERHEAD SAILS AWAY WITH THE FAMILY TREASURE, NICHOLAS CHASES AFTER HIM. BUT HE'LL NEED ALL HIS COURAGE TO OUTWIT CAPTAIN HAMMERHEAD'S SHARKS.

Also by Sherryl Clark
The Littlest Pirate

Happy Cat First Readers

The Littlest Pirate and the Hammerheads

Sherryl Clark

Illustrated by Tom Jellet

Published by
Happy Cat Books
An imprint of Catnip Publishing Ltd
14 Greville Street
London EC1N 8SB

First published by Penguin Books, Australia, 2005

This edition first published 2006
3 5 7 9 10 8 6 4

A CIP catalogue record for this book is available
from the British Library

ISBN 978-1-905117-27-7

Printed in Poland

www.catnippublishing.co.uk

Chapter One

'Achooo! Achooo!' Nicholas Nosh, the littlest pirate in the world, blew his nose and sniffed.

Gretta, chief cook and Nicholas's first mate, put down a bowl of chicken

soup. 'I told you swimming would make you sick. Pirates don't swim. They sail ships on *top* of the water.'

Nicholas sniffed again and grinned. 'You could just call me Nicholas Fish.'

'Hmmph!' Gretta stood up. 'I'd better get back to the kitchen. Your brother's birthday party is giving me a big headache.' Gretta had been cooking for the party for days – chocolate cakes, lemon tarts and a special chicken dish with olives and onions. Nicholas was

sorry to be missing out on
the feast, but he felt awful.
And he was totally, utterly
sick of chicken soup!

After Gretta left, he listened to the far-off sounds of people laughing and music playing. But it wasn't long before all was quiet again.

'Hmm,' said Nicholas. 'The party has ended early. I wonder why.' Then he fell asleep.

In the morning, all he could hear was lots of strange groaning.

He got out of bed, feeling much better, and went to investigate.

'Great gobstoppers!' Nicholas said in amazement. Pirates lay in the corridors, moaning and holding their stomachs. More pirates sprawled across the tables in the banquet hall. In their bedroom, Nicholas's mum and dad huddled under

their blankets, looking very ill.

'Have you all caught my cold?' Nicholas asked.

'No,' groaned his dad.

'It's Gretta's cooking. She's banned from the kitchen forever! Ooohhhh, I'm going to be sick again.'

Nicholas raced down to the kitchen. Something funny was going on. Gretta often had disasters with her cooking, but she'd never, ever made anyone ill.

In the kitchen, Gretta sat at the table, head in hands, crying.

'Gretta? What happened?' Nicholas asked.

'They all think I poisoned

them!' Gretta said miserably. 'It wasn't me, I know it wasn't. There was nothing wrong with my chicken.'

'Ooohh, what chicken?' moaned a maid who sat in the corner slumped over a large bowl. 'I thought you cooked beef curry. That's what we all ate.'

'I never made curry. I hate curry!' said Gretta.

Nicholas looked around the kitchen, then checked outside the back door. A large black pot with a few green mushrooms sat by the rubbish bin. 'Aha!' he said. 'Where did this come from?' He scrubbed the side of the pot and found a strange mark stamped in the metal.

Chapter Two

Gretta peered over Nicholas's shoulder. 'What's that funny mark?'

'Everyone has been poisoned,' said Nicholas. 'But not by you, Gretta. This is the mark of Captain

Hammerhead. I wonder . . .'

Nicholas raced up the stairs and into his family's treasure room. It was just

as he'd thought. The three largest chests were missing. All that was left were some silver cups and plates and two bolts of gold cloth. 'We've been robbed,' said Nicholas. 'We have to chase Hammerhead and get our treasure back.'

But when he ran back downstairs to round up a pirate crew, they were all too sick to move. Even

Nicholas's brother and sister just groaned and threw up again. Finally, after he'd searched high and low all around the village, he found just six pirates who could still walk – but only if they were helped.

Gretta was ready to sail. 'It's too bad if we're shorthanded,' she said. 'I'll be one of the crew. We can

live on sandwiches.' She thrust a cutlass and a pistol into her belt. She looked very, very mean.

They set sail in Nicholas's

very own ship, the *Golden Pudding*. Nicholas tied one pirate to the wheel to steer and put a bucket beside him just in case he was ill. Gretta and Nicholas ran up and down the ratlines, trimming the sails. The other sick pirates tried to help with the ropes when they weren't throwing up over the side of the ship.

Early the next morning,

Nicholas spied a ship in the distance. 'It must be Hammerhead's ship, the *White Fang*. How many

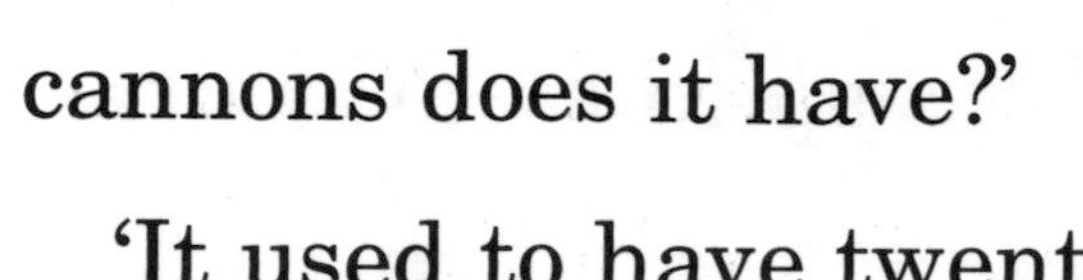

cannons does it have?'

'It used to have twenty,' Gretta said. 'But that ship looks a lot bigger . . .'

'We can take it,' Nicholas said confidently. 'Our pirates are feeling better now.' He ordered everyone to load their pistols and get the cannons ready. The *White Fang* was getting closer.

Gretta frowned. 'Um, I think – '

Boom! Boom! Boom! The *White Fang* fired all of its port-side cannons. Cannon

balls flew all around
the *Golden Pudding*
and one made a big
hole in the main sail.
Nicholas turned pale.

'That's not the
White Fang,' he said.
'It says *Deadly Denture*
on the side. But it's flying
Hammerhead's flag.
He must have captured
another ship.'

'It's twice as big,' said

Gretta. 'Forty cannons. And what's that shiny thing on the deck?'

Nicholas looked through his spyglass and his heart

sank. 'That's Captain Hammerhead. He's laughing and the sun is

shining off his bright silver teeth. We'd better retreat.'

The *Golden Pudding* moved out of range and Nicholas watched the *Deadly Denture* sail away. 'We'll follow,' he said. 'There must be a way to get our treasure back.'

Chapter Three

For three whole days, they followed Hammerhead's ship, watching and waiting. On the third day, Nicholas discovered something very scary. Four hammerhead sharks swam alongside

the huge ship.

Gretta trembled when she saw the sharks. 'Maybe we should give up,' she said. 'If our ship goes down . . .'

'We can't give up,' said Nicholas. 'Everyone at home is counting on us. I have some ideas, but we need Hammerhead to drop anchor first.'

Finally the *Deadly Denture* reached a large island and anchored in the bay. Pirates rowed ashore for fresh water. Through

his spyglass, Nicholas saw
the sun glinting off
Hammerhead's teeth as he
ordered his men to mend

sails and scrub decks. At dusk, they rolled out four barrels of rum and had a big party.

Nicholas noted two lookouts on deck and four shark fins circling the ship. ‘What’s in our food stores?’ he asked Gretta.

‘There’s not much left,’ said Gretta. ‘Fish cakes, liver, peanut butter . . .’

‘Yuck – but perfect,’ he said. ‘Mix that into balls. Now, I need the toolbox.’

He took a lantern down to the hold and found what

he wanted. It was time to put his plan into action.

'Lower the longboat,' he ordered the pirates. 'Gretta, can you row?'

'Of course.'

'Then you can row me to Hammerhead's ship,' Nicholas said.

'Are you crazy?' Gretta shouted.

'No. And bring those liver balls, please.'

While Gretta rowed, Nicholas crouched in the stern. When they were quite close, Nicholas slipped into the water before the lookouts saw him.

'Start throwing those balls into the water,' he

whispered, 'then row back to the *Golden Pudding*.'

Gretta was about to argue, but instead she tossed two balls into the sea and started rowing backwards. Nicholas swam to his left and waited. A few minutes later, he saw four black fins speed through the water and four big mouths snap at Gretta's liver balls.

As she threw more out,
the sharks followed her,
fighting and gnashing at

each other. Nicholas quietly paddled towards the *Deadly Denture*. When he reached the hull, he took a large drill out of his belt and carefully drilled six big holes. Water rushed in and soon the ship began to list to one side. He swam back towards the *Golden Pudding*.

Were the sharks still eating liver balls? Or would

a black fin slice through the water towards him at any moment?

Chapter Four

Just when Nicholas thought he saw a shark, Gretta and the pirates threw down a rope and hauled him back on board.

'Jiggling jellyfish!' said one pirate. 'I've never seen

anyone swim before.'

'Could come in handy,' said another.

Nicholas shivered – he'd

made it! They all stood at the rail and watched as the *Deadly Denture* slowly sank.

The sharks circled back. The liver balls had been a snack. Now maybe they'd get a main course!

At first, Hammerhead's pirates didn't realise what was happening. They slid across the deck and piled up against each other. Then

someone looked over the side and shouted a warning. 'We're sinking! Abandon ship!'

It was too late to save

anything. In a mad scramble, they lowered their longboats and climbed in. They rowed to the island and stood on the sand.

Hammerhead stayed with his ship. He stood on the deck, shouting, 'Come back, you scurvy lot!'

As the water rose, he climbed the main mast until he stood on the crow's nest. The *Deadly Denture* settled on the bottom of the bay, water halfway up its masts.

'Hmm,' said Nicholas. 'I thought he'd leave with his crew.'

Instead, Hammerhead tied himself to the mast with a rope and pulled out his cutlass. 'You can't have my treasure,' he yelled.

'It's not your treasure, it's mine!' Nicholas shouted

back. He wasn't going to give up now. He turned to Gretta. 'What have we got left in the galley?'

'Barely a thing,' said

Gretta. 'A big jar of garlic and some ship's biscuits that are as hard as rocks.'

'Great! Now, Gretta, I need to borrow something from you.' Nicholas whispered in Gretta's ear and she turned bright red.

'Nicholas!' she said, but she went below to fetch what he wanted.

Soon Nicholas was rowing back towards the

Deadly Denture.

Hammerhead stood on the crow's nest, cutlass ready. 'Haarrrr, you can't beat me with a cutlass,' he growled. 'You're just a puny little kid.'

Nicholas ignored him. When he was close enough,

he pulled out the elastic he'd borrowed from Gretta's undies. He made a slingshot and picked up a biscuit.

Ker-boing! Ker-boing! A biscuit hit Hammerhead in the belly. Another one hit him on the elbow. 'Ow! Stop that! That's not fair,' Hammerhead cried.

Nicholas aimed again. *Ker-BOING!* A big biscuit

hit Hammerhead right between the eyes and knocked him out. His

hammer hat fell into the water, revealing a little bald pointy head.

'Bull's eye!' said Nicholas. He rowed closer to check that Hammerhead wasn't moving. Nicholas jumped onto the crow's nest and tied the pirate up tightly with his own rope. Now to dive down for the treasure. There was no time to lose. The tide was coming in.

Suddenly four black fins appeared. The sharks were back.

Chapter Five

Nicholas picked up the jar of garlic and held his nose as he smeared it all over his body. When he jumped into the water, the sharks closed in, big jaws opening. Their teeth looked even bigger than Hammerhead's.

Nicholas wanted to shut his eyes but he couldn't. Instead he sang his

favourite pirate song to make him feel braver.

I love silver, I love gold,
I love treasure in my hold.
I love to sail the seven seas,
But I hate eating fat green peas.

The sharks swam closer and closer. Their mouths opened, showing razor-like teeth. Then their big hammer noses wrinkled up at the smell of the garlic. They flicked their tails and swished away.

Nicholas held his breath and dived. Down, down, down, through an open hatch and into the hold. Little fish darted around him. There were his treasure chests, just as he'd hoped, and another one as well. But they were far too

heavy to lift. In the deep water, he couldn't even move them a little.

He swam back to his boat and rowed to the *Golden*

Pudding. What were they to do? Everyone sat on the deck, head in hands, thinking hard.

'Could we pull the ship into shallow water?' said one pirate, flexing his muscles.

'It's too big,' said another. 'Even if we got that scurvy crew on shore to help.'

Hammerhead's pirates were still stuck on the island.

Nicholas's eyes sparkled. 'We won't pull the ship in,' he said. 'Just the chests.

But we'll need help.'

They rowed ashore holding a white flag of truce. Hammerhead's pirates soon agreed to help in return for some treasure. With four long ropes, in four big tug-of-war teams, they pulled the *Deadly Denture* over on its side.

'Oi, oi!' shouted Hammerhead. 'Get me down from here!' He hung

over the water like shark bait, but no one wanted to rescue him.

Nicholas dived again, hoping the garlic hadn't

worn off. The sharks circled slowly, their big noses wrinkling up. He tied the

ropes around the chests. Back on the beach, the pirates pulled again and slowly the chests were dragged out through the hatch and onto the sand.

'Yaayy!' shouted the pirates. 'We're rich!'

Nicholas pulled out his cutlass. 'Er, no, most of that treasure is mine, so hands off!'

'All right, all right,'

grumbled the pirates. 'No need to get your knickers in a knot.'

'No, only Gretta has to do that,' said Nicholas with a grin. He gave Gretta back her undies elastic.

They loaded up the *Golden Pudding*. Hammerhead's pirates all decided to join Nicholas's crew. But what to do about Hammerhead, who was still

tied to the mast? The tide was nearly up to his nose. Black fins cut through the water towards him.

'Please, please, I'm very,

very sorry. Save me!' he cried, tears dripping into the water. 'I'll do anything!'

Nicholas frowned. 'Shall we forgive him?'

‘Oh, very well,’ said Gretta. ‘He can work in the galley with me, but he’ll have to do all the dishes. And he’s not allowed to make any more curry!’

So Nicholas and his new crew sailed home with the treasure. His parents were so pleased they had a big party just for him, with lots of cake and lollies – and no chicken soup!

From Sherryl Clark

The idea for this new Nicholas Nosh story came from my sister-in-law, Bev. She went scuba diving in New Guinea a few years ago and found herself swimming with about twenty hammerhead sharks!

From Tom Jellett

I was surprised to find out how much sharks dislike garlic. Does this mean most hammerhead sharks don't like eating Italian food? Or do they just skip the garlic bread when they order pizza?

Look out for these other Happy Cat First Readers.

Nobody is better at being bad than Buster Reed – he flicks paint, says rude words to girls, sticks chewing gum under the seats and wears the same socks for weeks at a time. Naturally no one wants to know him. But Buster has a secret – he would like a friend to play with. How will he ever manage to find one?

Tom was given a gorilla suit for his birthday. He loved it and wore it everywhere. When mum and dad took him to the zoo he wouldn't wear his ordinary clothes. But isn't it asking for trouble to go to the zoo dressed as a gorilla?

No one believes in unicorns any more. Except Princess Lily, that is. So when the king falls ill and the only thing that can cure him is the magic of a unicorn, it's up to her to find one. But can Lily find a magical unicorn in time?

Becky was cross with her little brother. 'If you don't leave me alone,' she said to him, 'I'll put a spell on you!' But she didn't mean to make him disappear!

Nicholas Nosh is the littlest pirate in the world. He's not allowed to go to sea. 'You're too small,' said his dad. But when the fierce pirate Captain Red Beard kidnaps his family, Nicholas sets sail to rescue them!

Crystal longs to be a mermaid.
Her mother makes her a flashing silver tail. But it isn't like being a proper mermaid. Then one night Crystal wears her tail to bed...

Josie is Anna's best friend. Anna has played at Josie's house, she's even stayed for dinner, but she has never slept over. Until now…